P9-DYE-973

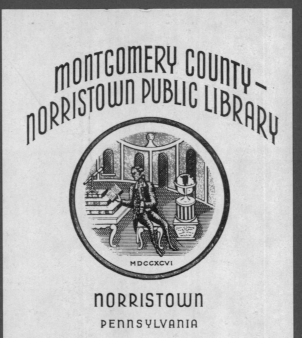

PLEASE WASH YOUR HANDS BEFORE HANDLING

Betty Lou Blue

Nancy Crocker ❄ pictures by Boris Kulikov

 Dial Books for Young Readers

To Grace, the Charlies, Rose, Paul, Claude,
and all my other guardian angels
—N.C.

To my wife
—B.K.

DIAL BOOKS FOR YOUNG READERS
A division of Penguin Young Readers Group
Published by The Penguin Group
Penguin Group (USA) Inc., 375 Hudson Street, New York, NY 10014, U.S.A.
Penguin Group (Canada), 90 Eglinton Avenue East, Suite 700, Toronto, Ontario, Canada M4P 2Y3 (a division of Pearson Penguin Canada Inc.)
Penguin Books Ltd, 80 Strand, London WC2R 0RL, England
Penguin Ireland, 25 St. Stephen's Green, Dublin 2, Ireland (a division of Penguin Books Ltd)
Penguin Group (Australia), 250 Camberwell Road, Camberwell, Victoria 3124, Australia (a division of Pearson Australia Group Pty Ltd)
Penguin Books India Pvt Ltd, 11 Community Centre, Panchsheel Park, New Delhi - 110 017, India
Penguin Group (NZ), Cnr Airborne and Rosedale Roads, Albany, Auckland 1310, New Zealand (a division of Pearson New Zealand Ltd)
Penguin Books (South Africa) (Pty) Ltd, 24 Sturdee Avenue, Rosebank, Johannesburg 2196, South Africa
Penguin Books Ltd, Registered Offices: 80 Strand, London WC2R 0RL, England

Text copyright © 1995, 2006 by Nancy Crocker
Pictures copyright © 2006 by Boris Kulikov
Portions of the text of this book were previously published in 1995 in *Once Upon a Time* in the story "Betty Lou Blue"
The publisher does not have any control over and does not assume any responsibility for author or third-party websites or their content.
Designed by Teresa Kietlinski Dikun
Text set in Adobe Garamond
Manufactured in China on acid-free paper

10 9 8 7 6 5 4 3 2 1

Library of Congress Cataloging-in-Publication Data
Crocker, Nancy.
Betty Lou Blue / Nancy Crocker ; pictures by Boris Kulikov.
    p. cm.
Summary: Teased by other children because of her big feet, only
Betty Lou can save her tormenters one snowy day.
ISBN 0-8037-2937-5
[1. Bullies—Fiction. 2. Foot—Fiction. 3. Stories in rhyme.]
I. Kulikov, Boris, date, ill. II. Title.
PZ8.3.C8738Bet 2006
[E]—dc22   2005036731

The artwork was created using mixed medium.

Betty Lou Blue had the world's biggest feet.
Whackety, thwackety, flappety feet.

The other kids laughed
 when she whappeted by.
"If those feet were wings," they would yell,
 "you could fly!"
"If those shoes were boats,
 you could float for a year!"
But whackety-flap, she'd pretend not to hear.

Her mama would rock her and say, "Betty Lou,
why, everyone's perfect, dear—
        yes, even you!
There's no one just like you—
            you're special, you see.
And each living thing has a reason to be."
So Betty Lou smiled,
        and tried to be strong,
But she knew in her heart that her mama was wrong.

Then the first day of winter,
    it started to snow;
Up came the wind,
    and it started to blow.
All morning long,
    the snow fell and it blew
Till the roads were all covered
    and hidden from view.

The principal let kids out early that day;
And said, "You go home!
Don't you dare stop to play!"

But outside the kids found a glorious sight—
  The park was a wonderland, sparkling white.
They all built a snowman
    and sledded
      and slid
    And some dared the others to do what *they* did;
But none of them noticed the tree by the street
    had seemingly sprouted
      two very large feet.

Betty Lou Blue was behind the tree, hiding,
And watching the building
and sledding
and sliding,
And wanting so badly to join in and play,
But she knew they'd just laugh
and then shoo her away,
Or join Jimmy Jack in his joke of the week,
Shouting, "Look, everybody,
it's Footy Lou Freak!"

So she watched the kids frolic
                and stayed out of sight,
And held back a gasp when they started to fight.
                One little snowball
                    was all that it took—
(Well, that and a shove and a menacing look).
                It quickly turned into an all-out attack
                With girls hitting boys
                        and boys fighting back.

They wrangled and rolled

and they wrestled until . . .

Betty Lou stepped out and yelled, "There's a hill!

Look out!" and they did, but a second too late.

The snow started shifting beneath all the weight.

They slid

and they tumbled

and fell

in a heap,

Then couldn't get up,

'cause the snow was too deep!

Frightened and frozen, they hadn't a clue
As to what could be done,
      till they saw Betty Lou.

The kids who had teased her
now shouted out, "Please!
Help us out of the snow! See, it's way past our knees!"
And Betty Lou stood there and studied the scene
While she thought about those
who had fun being mean.

Name-callers, bullies,
    that boy Jimmy Jack—
        Now here was her chance to pay them all back.
    And all it would take
        was her walking away—
Though Betty Lou knew what her mama would say.

"Dear, everything's ugly

    that's done out of spite;

        But you can be beautiful doing what's right.

'Cause what makes you special,

    what sets you apart,

Is not on the outside—it's there in your heart."

She looked the crowd over
    and stopped eye to eye
        With Jimmy Jack Jones, who had started to cry;
And a thought came to her
    that was ever so grim—
        Why, if I walk away, I'm as ugly as him.
So she made herself smile and she lifted her chin,
    And said,
        "Hey, come *on*, guys! It's time to go in!"

She knew what to do.
        It was really a cinch—
On top of the snow,
        without sinking an inch,
        She stood each kid up
            on the world's biggest feet
And walked each one out
        to the newly plowed street.

They hugged her and cheered,
  but the best part was when
All of them asked her
  to be their best friend.

Then she flappeted home in the darkening night
And burst in yelling,

"Mama, guess what! You were right!"

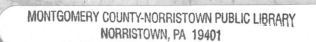